SCARED STIFF
and Other Creepy Tales

FOR MY MOM

SCARED STIFF
and Other Creepy Tales

By Andrew Helfer
Illustrated by Linda Medley

A GOLDEN BOOK • NEW YORK
Western Publishing Company, Inc., Racine, Wisconsin 53404

4

A Ball of String

Every day Brenda would read a book during the bus ride home from school. One day the book she read was so interesting that she missed her stop.

When Brenda got off the bus, everything looked strange and different. There were no stores on the streets. There were no cars. There were no people. Brenda felt alone and scared.

5

Then she heard footsteps around a corner.
Brenda ran toward the sound. She hoped she
would find someone who could show her the way
home.

Instead, Brenda bumped into a strange old
woman.

"Watch your step!" the old woman cackled. She wore a dirty torn coat and carried a big sack over her shoulder. Her teeth were cracked and yellow. She had a black patch over one eye.

"S-sorry," was all Brenda could say. She was too frightened by the old woman's face to ask for directions.

"Just don't let it happen again!" the old woman growled. As the old woman walked away, Brenda noticed something fall out of her coat pocket. It bounced down the street and stopped right by Brenda's feet. It looked like a ball.

Brenda picked it up. It was a strange kind of ball. It was made of thousands of bits of old and dirty string. The pieces had been tied together and wrapped into a ball.

8

Brenda held the ball in her hands. It felt warm.
She closed her hands around it and held it tight.
She thought she felt something move inside the
ball.

"There's something in the middle of this ball,"
Brenda thought. She felt a little scared.
"Something alive!"

Brenda looked at the sky. The sun was going
down. She had to get home before dark. She
walked quickly down the street. Every once in a
while the ball moved in her hands.

"There IS something alive in the middle of
this ball," Brenda thought. "And it wants to get
OUT!" she said aloud.

As she walked Brenda grabbed the end of the string and began to unwind it. She let the loose string fall to the ground. As she unwound more of the string, the ball became smaller. Her feeling that there was something in the middle of the ball grew stronger.

"What's inside this ball?" Brenda wondered. "Is it a mouse?" She shivered. Brenda didn't like mice. The ball got smaller.

"What if it is a creepy bug?" She liked bugs even less. The ball got smaller. "What if—" Then Brenda stopped wondering. She looked closely at the ball. A small piece of paper appeared, and on it was printed one word, "STOP!"

Brenda gulped. The ball twitched. Brenda unwound more string as she walked. The ball got smaller. Soon she came to another piece of paper. This one read "DON'T DO IT!"

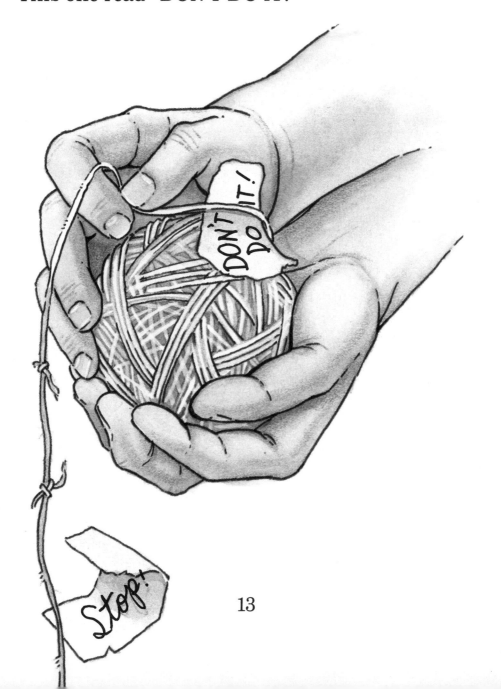

Brenda was really frightened now. She wanted to stop. She wanted to throw the ball away. But something made her continue. She unwound still more string. "UNWIND NO MORE!" the next piece of paper read. Now the ball was really small. It was not much bigger than a golf ball.

Brenda looked up. The sky was dark. How would she ever get home now. She wanted to cry. The ball jumped in her hand. She went back to unwinding the string. "YOU'RE DOOMED!" another piece of paper read.

The ball was very, very small now. Slowly, Brenda unwound the last bit of string. In the center of the ball was another ball. It shined in the moonlight. It was wet and cool. Brenda held it close to her face to get a better look.

IT WAS A HUMAN EYEBALL!

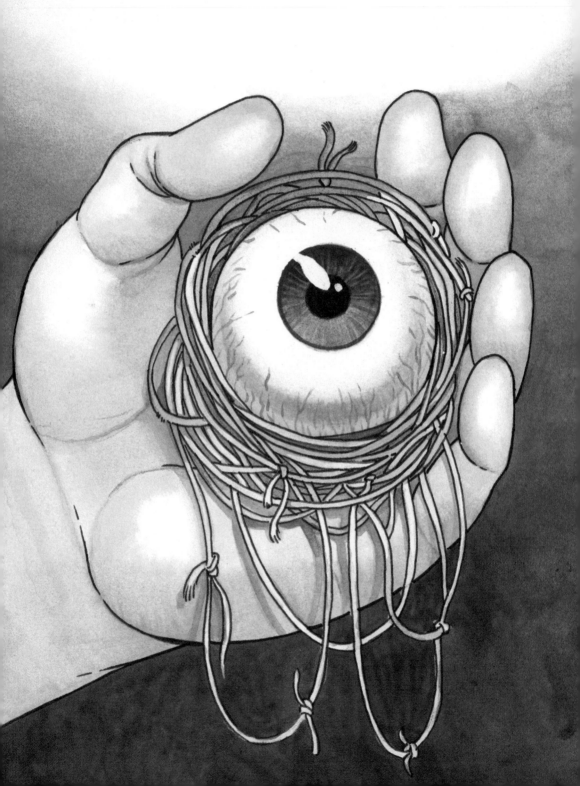

Brenda started to scream. A powerful hand
grabbed her by the shoulder and spun her
around.

17

"Can't you READ?!" the old woman screamed at Brenda. She reached over and snatched the eyeball out of Brenda's hand. Then she popped it into her head and stormed off.

18

Brenda was so frightened that she could hear her heart pounding in her head. She was all alone. She put her head in her hands and began to cry.

Then she heard a sound. It came from far away, but it was getting louder.

It sounded like…

...a bus!

The bus screeched to a halt in front of Brenda. The door opened, and the driver looked at Brenda. "What are you doing way out here all by yourself, little girl?" he asked.

"W-wishing I were home in bed!" Brenda replied in a shaky voice.

"Hop aboard," the driver said, and Brenda did. The door closed, and the bus rode off into the night.

In the Basement

Mike's father pointed proudly at the family's new home. "Isn't she a beauty?" he asked. Mike didn't think so. He thought the old house looked spooky. "No one has lived in this house for fifty years," Mike's father said. "I can't understand why!"

Mike understood why. The old house was probably haunted!

After he had unpacked, Mike decided it was time to explore. He walked through the big old house and explored every room. He looked inside every closet. There was nothing in any of them except cobwebs.

Soon there was only one place left to look…in the basement.

Mike opened the basement door and slowly walked down into the darkness. The old stairs groaned with each step he took. When he got to the bottom, Mike heard something move. He flashed his flashlight toward the sound. Then he saw it.

A monster! It was huge and furry, with bright red eyes that glowed in the darkness. Mike was frozen with fear. The monster didn't move either. But then, it seemed to smile. Mike could see its purple lips and big sharp teeth. It reached out toward Mike...

...and Mike raced up the stairs as fast as he could. He slammed the basement door behind him. Then he ran into the den, where his father was fixing a light.

"There's a monster in the basement!" Mike gasped.

"What an imagination you have!" his father said, chuckling. "It's probably just an old coat. But if it makes you feel better, I'll go take a look.

26

"Wait here," Mike's father said. "This will only take a minute."

Mike watched his father disappear into the basement. Then he listened. For a moment there was only silence. But then Mike heard a strange CHOMPING sound.

"Dad?" Mike whispered. "DAD?" But there was no answer.

Mike raced into the living room, where his mother was still busy unpacking.

"There's a monster in the basement!" Mike shouted. "And I think he's got DAD!"

Mike's mother smiled. "Your father is such a joker," she said. "He's probably hiding down there just to scare you!

"You wait right here," Mike's mother said at the top of the stairs. "These steps are old, and you might fall. I'll be right back." Then she walked into the darkness.

Mike waited. And waited. Long minutes passed. Then Mike heard a strange SLURPING sound.

"Mom?" he gasped. "MOM?" But there was no answer.

Mike raced up the stairs to his brother's room. His brother was listening to music.

"There's a monster in the basement!" Mike screamed. "And he's got Mom and Dad!"

"Yeah, right," Mike's brother said, laughing. "This I gotta SEE!" He got up and ran down the stairs toward the basement.

"Wait!" Mike shouted after him. "Don't go in there! If it got Mom and Dad, it'll get you too..." But it was too late. By the time Mike reached the basement door, his brother had already gone down the stairs.

Mike had no choice. He had to help his family. He turned his flashlight on and went back down into the basement.

At first Mike heard nothing. Then he heard a SLURPING sound. And a CHOMPING sound. And a terrible, horrible BURPING sound!

Mike gulped. The monster was EATING UP his family! He had to try to stop it!

Mike raised his flashlight toward the horrible sounds. He could not believe his eyes!

His entire family was sitting around a small table. They looked as though they had just finished EATING. His father was wiping his mouth. His mother was dusting some crumbs off her lap. His brother just smiled at Mike—and burped.

"You were RIGHT, Mike!" his mother said. "There WAS a monster in the basement...

"...but he's a very, very FRIENDLY monster!"

Scared Stiff

David loved scary movies. The scarier, the better. He liked to feel his spine tingle. He loved to feel his hair stand on end. And sitting on the edge of his seat was his favorite way to sit.

David kept searching for the scariest movie of all. One day, he found it. "The scariest time of your life!" read the sign in front of the theater. "Or double your money back!"

David bought a bag of popcorn and sat down to watch the movie. There were monsters. There were vampires. There were werewolves! David's eyes opened wide. The sign was right. This *was* the scariest movie he had ever seen.

David reached for the popcorn. But his hand would not move. He tried to look down but he could not move his eyes. "What is wrong with me?" David wondered. Then he understood. He was scared stiff.

Later, the movie theater was about to close for the night. David still sat quietly in his seat. He was the only customer left. The theater manager came up to David.

"I'm sorry, sir," the manager said, "the theater is closing for the night. You'll have to leave now." David didn't move. He COULDN'T move. He was scared stiff!

"Hmm," the manager said, "I think we'd better call the police."

Soon the police arrived. They shined a flashlight in David's eyes. Still David didn't move. "We'd better call for an ambulance," one policeman said.

Moments later, the paramedics came up to David. One of them waved a hand in front of David's face. "I would move if I could," David thought. "But I can't! I'm scared stiff!"

The paramedics picked David up and put him in an ambulance. "He's stiff as a board!" one of them said. "Poor guy," said the other. Then they rushed David off to the hospital.

In the hospital, the doctors examined David. They poked at him with needles, but David didn't feel a thing. "There's nothing I can do for this man," David heard one of the doctors say. Then someone put a white sheet over his face.

David wanted to cry out. But he couldn't. He was scared stiff.

David could see the sun in the sky above him.
People were looking down at him. They all looked
very sad. Some of these people were David's
friends and his family. He wanted to say hello.
But he couldn't. He was scared stiff.

Then a man came and closed a wooden lid over him. David heard the sound of nails being banged in. He felt himself being lowered into the ground. He heard dirt being thrown on the wood. Then he heard nothing.

Hours passed. David was frightened. He understood what had happened. Everyone thought he was dead. He had been buried alive. "But I'm not dead!" David thought. "I'm just scared stiff!

"I have to snap out of this!" David thought. David remembered about the movie. And he remembered the monsters. And the vampires. And the werewolves. David remembered that they weren't REALLY monsters and vampires and werewolves. They were only actors wearing makeup! "How silly to get scared stiff," David said, "by a bunch of actors!

"Hey!" David said suddenly. "I'm talking! I'm not scared stiff anymore! I've snapped out of it!" He began to kick and punch at the coffin lid. He screamed and shouted loud enough to wake the dead.

Soon, David heard digging above him. "Thank goodness!" David said. "Someone has come to rescue me!" In a little while, David heard the sound of a shovel hitting the coffin lid. "It won't be long now," David said.

46

"Thank you!" David began to shout as the lid of his coffin was raised. But once he saw who his rescuers were, David was more scared than ever.

"W-who are you?" David said, trembling.

"We are the Dead," one of them said. "You were screaming loud enough to wake us. We thought we'd let you out so we can go back to sleep."

With that, David leapt out of the coffin and went screaming off into the night.

One of the Dead looked down at David's coffin. "This one looks so comfortable," he said. "I wonder why he wanted to leave it so badly."